TWEED FICTION J

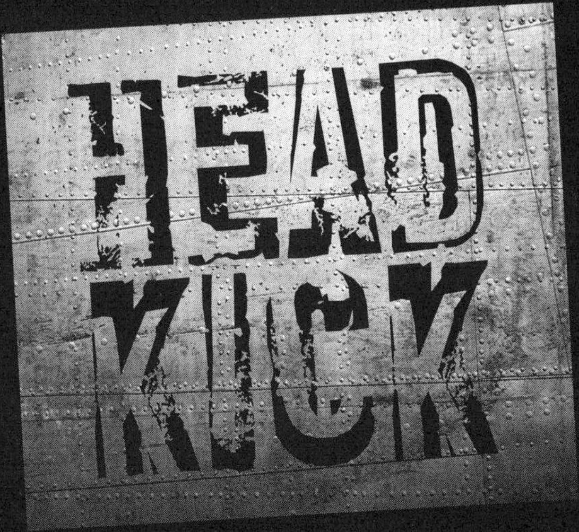
HEAD
KICK

HEAD KICK

BY PATRICK JONES

darbycreek

MINNEAPOLIS

Darby Creek
A division of Lerner Publishing Group, Inc.
241 First Avenue North
Minneapolis, MN 55401 U.S.A.

Website address: www.lernerbooks.com

The images in this book are used with the permission of: © Panorama Media/
Getty Images (fighter); © iStockphoto.com/Tim Messick (background);
© iStockphoto.com/Erkki Makkonen (metal wires); © iStockphoto.com/
TommL (punching fist), © iStockphoto.com/dem10 (barbed wire).

Main body text set in Janson Text LT Std 12/17.5.
Typeface provided by Linotype AG.

Library of Congress Cataloging-in-Publication Data

Jones, Patrick, 1961–
    Head kick / by Patrick Jones.
        pages   cm. — (The dojo ; #3)
    ISBN 978–1–4677–0632–2 (lib. bdg. : alk. paper)
    ISBN 978–1–4677–1633–8 (eBook)
    [1. Mixed martial arts—Fiction. 2. Family problems—Fiction.
3. Hmong Americans—Fiction.] I. Title.
PZ7.J7242He 2013
[Fic]—dc23   2012042249

Manufactured in the United States of America
1 – SB – 7/15/13

IN MEMORY OF
MILES KLEIN
-P.J.

WELCOME
TO
the
DOJO

If you're already a fan of mixed martial arts, in particular the Ultimate Fighting Championship (UFC), then you're probably familiar with moves like triangle choke, spinning heel kick, and Kimura. If not, check out the MMA terms and weight classes in the back of the book. You can also go online for videos of famous fights and training videos. Amateur fights are similar to the pros but require more protection for the fighters. While there are unified rules, each state allows for variation.

WELCOME TO THE DOJO.
STEP INSIDE.

CHAPTER 1

"*Ladies and gentlemen, your winner by knockout in twenty seconds, and your new UFC featherweight champion of the world, the Ninja Warrior, Nong Vang!*"

The Las Vegas crowd goes crazy as the referee raises Nong's powerful right arm. With his left hand Nong blows kisses to his legion of fans, including his girlfriend, May Li. Ring announcer Bruce Buffer hands the microphone to UFC broadcaster Joe Rogan.

"*That was almost a perfect fight,*" Rogan says to Nong. "*Your best since winning Ultimate Fighter.*"

"Thanks Joe," Nong replies. "Discipline in the dojo and aggression in the cage—that's the formula."

"That was one of the most devastating head kick knockouts I've ever seen. Tell me, which featherweight contender would you like to face at the next UFC pay-per-view?"

Nong laughs. "Joe, it doesn't matter who I face. They're not contenders, they're pretenders. I'm the Ninja Warrior power company, and my opponents don't pay their bills. So I put their lights out."

"Anyone you'd like to thank?"

"Of course, my coaches, Mr. Hodge and Mr. Matsuda. Also my training partners, Hector, Jackson, and Meghan. We walked into the Missouri MMA dojo together at age sixteen, and they've supported me since. Shout-out to my nephew Bao and all my love to May Li. I'm a champion tonight, baby!"

"And you will be for a long time. How does that feel?"

Nong smiles at the camera and points to his title belt. "Joe, it's like I'm living a dream."

CHAPTER 2

"Nong, pay attention!" Hector shouts at me.

I snap out of my daydream and focus on the action in the dojo. Everyone is paired up for a drill.

"Strike!" Mr. Hodge yells.

"Watch this!" I shout. As Hector gets set, I throw a spinning heel kick. It doesn't seem to faze Hector—he outweighs me by forty pounds, and the sparring helmet helps absorb the blow. In a real fight against another featherweight, the guy would be picking up his teeth with his left hand while the ref would be raising my right hand.

Hector counters with punches. He's got a boxing background, while I trained in karate and tae kwon do before we started MMA almost two years ago. He's powerful, but I'm faster.

"What's wrong, Hector? Can't catch the Ninja Warrior?"

Hector doesn't react, just keeps throwing punches. He's got a longer reach, so I close the distance using front and side kicks to his legs. I fake a head kick and counter with a left. Hector shakes it off. Using his weight and height advantage, he forces my head down with a Muay Thai clinch as he brings his knees up crashing.

"OK." I tap his arm, and Hector releases me. I throw an angry side kick at no one.

"Nong, you got a big mouth, and someday somebody's gonna shut it," Hector says.

"In your dreams, Hector." He grunts something like a laugh. Lately, getting Hector to laugh would be as impressive as knocking him out. He didn't always used to be so serious, but all of us are different than we were at sixteen. We tap gloves and spar again.

After a few minutes, Mr. Hodge stops the

drills. "Hector and Eric, into the ring!"

Eric is newer to the dojo, which means he's going to take a lot of punishment. It's how the "new fish" show they're tough enough. I stand next to the judo and jiu-jitsu coach, Mr. Matsuda, as Eric and Hector spar. Hector's a cat, while Eric's a ball of string. And Eric knows it. He's throwing punches, but he's not fighting. He's delaying the inevitable.

"I don't think Eric's going to make it," I whisper to Mr. Matsuda. He says nothing. As we watch, the silence is broken only by Mr. Hodge yelling instructions to each fighter and then explaining the calls to us.

Hector lands a vicious roundhouse kick on Eric's knee. "I taught him that," I say.

Again, Mr. Matsuda says nothing. He drums his fingers on his chin. I do the same. While Hector's kick did damage, he also lost his balance, and Eric takes him down. With his back on the mat, Hector fights off Eric's moves. "Flat on your back can be a great position, no?"

Mr. Matsuda nods his head absentmindedly. "Depends on the fighter and the fight."

"If this was my fight, here's what I'd do." I explain to Mr. Matsuda how Hector should use Eric's sloppy mount against him. "Hector needs to slip into rubber guard, execute a gogoplata or triangle choke, and then it's lullaby time for Eric."

Mr. Matsuda finally turns his attention to me. "Good plan, but everybody's got a good plan—"

"Until they get punched in the face," I finish one of Mr. Matsuda's favorite sayings, which he ripped off the boxer Mike Tyson.

The second round starts, and it's like Hector had been listening to our conversation. He gets taken down too easy but then slaps on a triangle choke. Eric taps.

After Hector and Eric climb from the ring, Mr. Matsuda takes them to the corner to drill. Meghan sidles over to me. "What do you think of these new fish?" she asks with a smirk. While Jackson and Hector are really serious, Meghan is funny and seems to have a life outside the dojo. *Seems to* because none of us knows much about her. *Seems to* because she practically lives at the dojo.

"Pretty green around the gills," I say. She laughs.

"Not everybody can be like you, Clark." Meghan calls me Clark Kent because I wear glasses outside of the dojo.

"I'm better than Superman. I'm the perfect MMA machine, the Ninja Warrior!"

"You're something else, Clark," she says, then taps me hard on my sore right shoulder.

"I'm soon to be UFC world featherweight champion!"

"Well, you know, after you turn eighteen, graduate from high school, go to college, and fight amateur for a while, then maybe—"

"Maybe I'll go pro right away."

Meghan raises an eyebrow. "Then you'd be like Eric." We watch as Mr. Matsuda instructs Hector on tying up Eric like a pretzel. "You'd be a drill dummy, Nong."

I shake my head and walk away. I walk to my locker, take out my phone, and watch a round of one of my favorite UFC fights. I go back into the dojo, head down so I don't glare at Meghan and everyone else. Alone in the corner, I jump rope, imagining myself in the fight, and let my reality drift away.

CHAPTER 3

May Li offers me a sushi roll as we stand in the school parking lot. I shake my head. "I need to stay within my weight class," I answer.

She readjusts her black-rim glasses, which look like mine. But glasses are about all we have in common: she's tall for a girl, while I'm short for a guy. She's brainy, I'm brawny. But the main thing that separates us is this: I dream about her, and I bet she doesn't even think about me.

"Nong, I don't see how you can fight like that. You seem so gentle."

I hide my disappointment. I've tried to get

her to call me "Ninja Warrior," but she just laughs. Just like I've tried to call her to ask her out, but I always choke. She'd probably laugh at that too. "Well, I don't see how you can study like that," I say, pointing at the stack of books in her bag.

"I guess everybody has things they're good at ... like this sushi chef!" She takes another bite. "Sometimes I wish I could forget about college and just train to be a chef."

"But you've gotta uphold the family tradition, right?" I ask. All of May Li's older brothers and sisters were star students: honor roll, AP classes, and academic scholarships.

"Something like that," she says. "Did your brothers go to college?"

"No. My oldest brother, Ywj, began our tradition of high school dropouts." Ywj, his wife Kia, and their son Bao just moved back to St. Louis from St. Paul. I missed Kia and Bao, but Ywj, not at all. I try to see Bao as much as I can; I avoid Ywj as much as humanly possible.

"I bet your parents were upset. I know mine would be."

"Not at all, actually," I say. "My dad told Ywj to act like a man after Ywj got Kia pregnant. So he dropped out, married Kia, and went to work. He just lost that job."

"So I guess you're starting a new family tradition by graduating."

I shrug my shoulders, which makes me wince in pain.

"You okay, Nong?"

I've tried to trick May Li various times into giving me back rubs, but it never works. "I'm fine. I just had a really good spar at the dojo last night."

"Maybe you should fight less and study more. I know you know how to study." My parents want me to graduate with a good GPA, so last year I asked May Li to tutor me in a few classes as her National Honor Society service project. She was a patient teacher.

"I study. I study MMA all the time," I say, and she laughs. "Name a move, and I'll tell you who used it to finish what fight, who they beat, and even which event."

"If only you could use those skills toward

school," she says. I can't tell if she's teasing. "Oh, I have to get home to practice violin," she says as she checks the time and throws the empty sushi container away. "See you tomorrow?"

"Bye," I say. As I head to my car, I realize how hungry I am and remember the dessert Mom put in the fridge.

*   *   *   *   *   *

I'll be coming home to an empty house. Mom and Dad have both worked two jobs since Dad lost his business. They don't really like my MMA career, but they do sacrifice to pay for it. In return I've promised them good grades, no drugs, no booze, and to avoid the Hmong gangs in our neighborhood.

My parents aren't there when I get home, but Ywj and his eight-year-old son, Bao, are sitting in the living room. Bao watches my dad's big TV while Ywj talks on his cell, his back to me. I don't make any effort to speak to Ywj, just like he never talks to Dad. But Bao turns around and greets me the way I taught him: "Uncle Ninja Warrior!"

I pick him up, spin him around, and then powerbomb him gently onto the sofa.

Bao laughs. "Do it again!" I lift him up and grant him his wish. He laughs loud and long, and I join in. Ywj remains on the phone. It sounds like he's talking to his wife, Kia.

"So, Bao, you decide on my birthday present yet?" I ask playfully. "It's only two months away!"

Bao just laughs more.

I head into the kitchen and see the message light flashing. My parents seem to have the only landline and answering machine left in the universe. There's a message from my cousin Lue. He also left messages on my cell, so it must be important. When I call him back, he's says he's on his way to his tae kwon do class so he can't talk long and wants to get right to the point.

"I want to start MMA training now that I'm sixteen. Are there spots in your teen program?"

I pause before I answer. For two years, I've succeeded in keeping my life divided: there's the Nong Vang that my school and family know, and there's the Ninja Warrior I am at the dojo.

If Lue joins the dojo, the distance between my worlds shrinks. "I'm not sure," I say.

"We'd make a great team: Lightning Lue and the Ninja Warrior!"

I pause again, this time distracted by a noise from the other room like something tipped over. That's followed by a door slam.

"OK, I'll call the dojo and ask. I bet I could learn a lot from you," Lue says before he hangs up.

I open the fridge and take out leftover tricolor dessert. I fill two bowls and overfill a third one for me, and head back into the living room. Bao is quiet this time, and Ywj is gone.

"Here, Mighty Bao." I put the bowl on the table near him. He sniffs like he's got a cold.

As he reaches for the tricolor treat, I see his tricolor face. His eyes are white, his pupils are brown, and his busted lip drips red blood, courtesy of his dad, my brother, our shared bully.

CHAPTER 4

While Jackson and Hector spar in the center mat, I practice drills with Shawn Hart. Shawn has yet to get Muay Thai training because he keeps missing evenings to play school sports.

"No, Shawn, you need to clasp your hands like this," I explain, threading my fingers together as I wrap my hands around his skinny white neck. "Understand?"

"Is that how Anderson Silva does it?" Shawn asks. Silva is the King of the Thai Clinch.

"Exactly!" I pull him tighter in the clinch. "Do it perfectly, and no one can escape."

Shawn tries the grip, but I slip out. I make him do it a few more times until he gets it right. Mr. Matsuda stops by to check on us. Or to give me a hard time.

"Is this really Silva's grip?" Shawn asks Mr. Matsuda and then puts me in the clinch.

"It doesn't matter," Mr. Matsuda says and glares at me. "When I started in MMA, I just wanted to be a fighter. I didn't copy someone else's moves. And I didn't give myself a nickname."

"Well, those ancient Greeks didn't have a lot of moves," I say. Shawn laughs, but Mr. Matsuda frowns at me. "Seriously, why not use cool moves from UFC?" I say.

"Cool moves don't win real fights, they just look good," Mr. Matsuda explains. "They might impress judges, but they don't impress me. Stick to the basics. Grapple, strike, submit."

"That doesn't sound like much fun," I say.

Another glare, this one harder. "Nong, who told you this was supposed to be fun?"

"This, oh, *this* is no fun at all, all these drills," I explain. "But once I get some fights under me, get on the Ultimate Fighter, win the contract, and get in the UFC, all that will be fun."

"Maybe you should think about winning the dojo spars more often first," Mr. Matsuda counters.

I look away. I know the coaches don't keep dojo win-loss records, or if they do, they hide them. But he's right. I'm on the losing side, mainly because most of the fighters in the dojo are bigger than me. Once I face someone my own weight and skill level, I'll show him.

"This is a sport of upsets," Shawn says to Mr. Matsuda, helping my case. "Even the most dominant fighter loses sometimes."

"Nong, if all you care about is being famous," Mr. Matsuda says sternly, "you'll never win a single amateur fight." As he walks away, I hear him mumble, "I wish TV and magazines never would've found this sport."

Shawn and I finish the drill, and then we turn toward a punching bag. "You know, I take it back—these drills *can* be fun," I say. "Master Hodge, look at this!" I shout as I show off some of my best moves on the punching bag: flying knees, spinning back fists, and standing savate kick.

"Nong, get serious!" Mr. Hodge shouts at me.

"I'm seriously ready to get into that cage!"

Mr. Hodge puts his hands on his hips. "Then stop screwing around."

"I'm not, I'm getting ready," I explain. "I watched Hector, and I knew what he was going to do. You always say the only way to win in this sport is to do the unexpected. Everybody knows you teach the ground-and-pound style, so that's what they'll be looking for. Well, I'll have a little surprise for them for sure." I throw a perfect roundhouse kick that rocks the top of the bag.

"You want to surprise us? All right, let's go, Nong," Hodge says and motions for me to come over. "Shawn, get in here."

We jog over to the center mat. Before I put in my mouth guard I shout, "Shawn, are you ready to take a nap?"

He doesn't respond. But before Shawn steps on the mat, Hodge whispers something in his ear. I put on my helmet, straighten my gloves, and bounce on my feet. Inside, it feels like the butterflies in my stomach are bouncing too.

"OK, let's do this!" Mr. Hodge yells, then blows a whistle.

I'm sure Mr. Hodge told Shawn to take me down, because I'm much weaker on the ground than on my feet, but I won't give him a chance. I don't bother to circle or throw jabs. I rush in and start with kicks to his legs and side. He blocks the kicks, but not the picture-perfect flying knee that crushes his chest. He staggers, and I rush my next move, but in doing so I lose my balance. Suddenly Shawn is on top in full mount, and he uses his legs to control me. Mr. Hodge blows the whistle.

A smiling Shawn gets up. He offers me a hand, but I ignore it and stare at the mat.

Mr. Hodge isn't happy. "Nong, someone in your weight class would have grounded and pounded you, but you grounded yourself. You can't give away anything—am I right?" I can only nod in agreement.

"All right, everybody here," Hodge says, gathering us in the center of the dojo. "As you know, we have four fighters almost ready to enter their first amateur competition. They'll be taking on fighters more experienced, but I guarantee you, not better trained. So, to get our fighters ready, I've organized a scrimmage of sorts. We'll take on fighters at the MMA Academy next week, and then the week after, they'll enter our cage."

"Who fights first?" I ask.

"Next week, you and Hector, and then Meghan and Jackson the week after."

I bump fists with Hector. Mr. Hodge talks more about the challenge of fighting people who don't know your strengths or weaknesses, but I'm not listening. I'm too busy hearing the cheers in my ears as I imagine my devastating victory.

CHAPTER 5

"Nong, do you want more chicken?" my mom asks as she pushes the plate toward me.

"I told you, I have a fight in two days. I just barely made weight today."

"You could stand to gain a few pounds," Mom says.

"He always was the runt of the litter," Dad says and laughs too hard. People say that lies hurt, but the truth hurts worse. I'm almost eighteen but still weigh less than 145 pounds. My older brothers, Ywj, Tha, and Vam, were bigger than me at this age. And none of them were athletes, unless beating up their little brother counts as a sport. Even Ywj's wife, Kia, is bigger than me.

"I'm not a runt," I say. "I'm a Ninja Warrior."

"Whoever you are, eat!" Dad scolds. I take the smallest leg and pull off the greasy skin. Dad puts the biggest piece of chicken left on his plate. "Kia wanted to have dinner with us because she had something to give you," he says to me. "But she said Bao was sick."

"Bao seems to get sick a lot since they moved back here," I say softly.

"She dropped off the present and wants you to call her," Mom says. I nod and pick at the meat.

"So, we can't see your fight?" Dad asks. "I'd love to tape it to show the guys at work."

"No, Mr. Hodge doesn't want families or friends at the dojo. He says it distracts."

"Then get one of the other fighters to video it for me," Dad demands, as if I should've thought of that. I give another nod.

"It won't be much of a fight," I say. "I'll take him out in less than a minute, I predict."

"You've got such confidence and aggression. I don't know where it comes from," Mom says to me, although she shoots Dad a look.

I don't answer. Instead I finish my salad, all the while staring at the remaining chicken. My stomach's in a civil war: half of it empty with hunger, the other half full with anxiety.

* * * * *

After dinner, Dad and I go into the living room. He smokes, and I roll my wrists like Wanderlei Silva used to do. Everybody's got their habits to work out their nerves.

"How's school going?" he asks.

"It's hard."

"Anything important is hard," Dad says. "If it's easy, it's not worth doing."

"Thank you, wise old owl." I bow my head and then break out in laughter. Dad joins in.

"What's so funny?" Mom asks as she walks in with a present under her arm.

"Nothing," I say. "What's that?"

"This is from Kia. Remember, she wants you to call her when you open it."

I pull out my phone and call Kia. She answers, but there's a lot of noise in the background. It sounds like Bao is crying. I have a pretty good idea why.

"I embroidered something for you," Kia says. Embroidery is one of her part-time jobs. "Go ahead and open it."

"Thanks, Kia." I rip open the wrapping paper. There's a gold robe with the words *Ninja Warrior* stitched in black on the back of it. "Kia, it's great. I don't know what to say."

"You don't need to say anything. Good luck in your fight."

"Put it on!" Dad says. I don the robe. It feels right.

"Send me some pictures, okay?" Kia asks.

"Sure. Thanks again, Kia." I hang up and hand my phone to Mom. I explain to her for the hundredth time how to take a picture. As the camera flashes, I imagine it's photographers surrounding me before my first UFC fight. I'm not the runt of the litter; I'm the Ninja Warrior. I am strong and fearless.

I send the photos to Kia. I think about

sending them to other people at the dojo but decide against it. None of them except maybe Meghan seem to realize that while MMA is a sport, it's also a show. The best fighters possess skills, courage, and charisma. I decide to send the best photo to May Li, too, and I wonder when I'll find the skill and courage to ask her out.

⌷ ⌷ ⌷ ⌷ ⌷

Like most nights, I head down to the basement to work out. My dad bought me a secondhand weight set, and Lue's father, Uncle Huaj, gave me some martial arts training gear that Lue was finished using. While I lift, I think about how it would be if Lue joined our dojo. Like me, he's done karate and tae kwon do since he was a kid. When we were smaller, we trained together. But he got bigger while I stayed small.

After a strong workout and a shower, I head back to my room and look at my phone. There are missed calls from Hector and Jackson and some texts from Kia commenting on the pictures, but nothing from May Li. I know she tutored me last year for NHS service points, but I could tell she enjoyed helping me. Once I retire from MMA, I'd maybe like to help people in the same way. I open my physics book and use some of the tricks I worked on with May Li to review what we did in class and finish the homework.

I end the night studying the arts: mixed martial arts. I bring the laptop over to the bed, click on the MMA folder, and open a can of Mountain Dew. I have thousands of files nicely organized. If studying for school was more like studying MMA, I'd ace all my classes.

I open the file "Head Kick KOs" and watch some of the greatest kicks in MMA history. Many feature Mirko Cro Cop, the retired Croatian heavyweight Pride fighter, who threw one of the most devastating head kicks in the sport.

After each fight, I close my eyes and try to visualize me in Cro Cop's bare feet. I see how he sets up each kick with other strikes and how he uses feints to fake out his foes. I listen to the commentary as the announcer raves about Cro Cop's perfect technique.

I'm deep into the fights when a message from May Li pops up.

"Thanx 4 pix," it says.

I pause to think of something funny to say back, but it's too late. She's offline before I can answer. When I return to the videos, it's Cro Cop vs. Gabriel Gonzaga from UFC 70. Cro Cop was a huge favorite, and the bout was thought to be just a tune-up before he got his first UFC heavyweight championship match. It's tough to watch what really happened. Gonzaga destroyed Cro Cop on the ground with elbows and then, after the stand-up, finished him with the head kick knockout. Cro Cop was never the same after this fight. One humiliating loss turned a once-unbeatable superman into a normal fighter filled with doubt.

I turn off the computer and head to bed. I close my eyes, visualizing my upcoming amateur fight. I see myself, the Ninja Warrior, as Cro Cop—the Cro Cop from Pride; not the one with his pride taken from him by Gabriel Gonzaga. I plan out my moves in the cage and imagine the roar of the crowd. But as the scene blends into my dreams, an unsettled feeling flickers through my mind.

CHAPTER 6

"I'm not feeling well," I tell Mr. Hodge just before I climb into his car to go to the scrimmage. I had wanted to say I couldn't make the fight because I was sick, but my dad said I looked okay to him, and besides, if I was as good as I claimed, I wouldn't even need to be 100 percent to win.

"That's just nerves, you'll be fine," Mr. Hodge says. I climb in the backseat next to Hector. Hector just stares at the back of the seat. I try to talk with him, but he's not having it.

"So, Mr. Hodge, tell me about your first fight," I say.

"You should be thinking about your fight, not mine."

"I am." My stomach churns again. "But I'm also thinking of the first MMA fight I ever saw." I tell Mr. Hodge what I remember so vividly, stumbling across MMA on television when I was six. It became my refuge. After one of my brothers would bully me, I'd watch MMA and pretend I was one of the fighters. I guess, in some ways, I never grew out of that.

"Nong, shut up," Hector hisses, but I don't listen.

The MMA Academy is bigger than our dojo. "We can warm up over there," Mr. Hodge says.

We're already in our fighting clothes. Mr. Hodge and Mr. Matsuda didn't tell me not to wear Kia's robe, but I know from their frowns and furrowed brows that they'd prefer I not. I take the robe off when Jackson, Meghan, and Mr. Matsuda arrive.

Jackson holds up a blocker, and I start warming up, throwing hard strikes. He's encouraging me while Mr. Hodge goes over the game plan. I'll start with jabs and then, as he puts his hands up, I'll move to leg kicks. When he drops his hands to defend, it'll open up the head kick. If I'm on the ground, I'll look for a choke submission.

"Nong, you're up first," Mr. Hodge says. Jackson and Mr. Hodge follow behind as I start toward the cage. Shawn and some other fighters from our dojo sit in folding chairs, applauding. It's only a few hands clapping, but I imagine a huge roar.

The fighter from the MMA Academy enters the cage, followed by one of his coaches. My opponent, Alex Taylor, is a muscular white kid with a wrestler's body. He'll kill me on the mat, so I need to avoid his takedowns. As the MMA Academy ref gives us instructions, I close my eyes, visualize the fight, and become the Ninja Warrior.

"Gentlemen, you know the rules. You'll be fighting three two-minute rounds. If there is no clear winner, I will act as the judge to decide one. Obey my instructions at all times. Protect yourselves, and have a good fight. Let's make this happen." *Let's make it quick* is all I can think.

We touch gloves and return to our corners until a whistle blows. I charge out and start throwing jabs. He returns with punches of his own, but neither of us connects. He's in the center of the cage, circling me. I step forward, and he answers with a strong front kick. He tries to clinch and throw knees, but I slip out and get distance. I connect with a low kick and follow with a solid left jab. When he tries a takedown, I defend with more kicks: head, body, and one that cracks loud against his left elbow.

"Work the plan!" I hear Mr. Hodge yell.

I fake an overhand left and a takedown. I follow up with more leg kicks. He's still circling, but he's limping. He dives for a double leg. I sprawl, looking for a choke, but he defends it well, so I push away. He's better than I thought, or maybe I'm worse.

When I try for a head kick, he grabs my left leg, shoulders into me, and takes me down. I close guard, but he hits hard with elbows from his right arm. He tries his left, but I grab it and pull him toward me, looking for an arm lock.

"Alex, stick him!" his corner yells.

From half guard, he throws knee after knee into my side. He's really got me jammed against the cage. I hear Mr. Hodge yelling something, but I can't concentrate with these elbows smashing against my face. Mr. Hodge yells again, but I hear only the sound of people laughing at me as I'm getting dominated. I make a panicked attempt to escape, but in doing so, I give him my back. He locks in the rear naked choke.

"Ten seconds," I hear. Two seconds later I tap out in the first round.

We both stand and tap gloves, and the ref raises my opponent's hand. I hug him as a show of respect. He takes out his mouthpiece. "Those are some mean kicks," he says.

"Alex Taylor, I predict that one day you'll be a famous fighter."

"Thanks, but—" he starts, but I cut him off.

"As the fighter that got lucky and beat future UFC champ Nong 'Ninja Warrior' Vang!"

"You're cocky for a guy who just got beat," Alex says. I don't disagree. As I walk out of the cage, I recall something I heard once in history class: the bigger the lie, the more people believe it.

CHAPTER 7

"Are you hurt?" May Li asks. We're walking home from school on the first nice day we've had in months.

I point to the small cut over my eye. "You should see the other guy."

She laughs. "I'd be so afraid of getting hurt."

I shrug. The hurt goes away, but the humiliation of losing stays like some huge stone around my neck. Just like how the old bruises from the poundings my brothers gave me in the past have healed. But the panic and terror, I doubt they'll ever go away.

"Well, I admire you for having so much determination to do something like that."

"Well, you do the same with studying, right?" I ask. She nods and smiles. "I just don't do so good with the alphabet. The only two letters I care about are *K* and *O*."

"OK," she says. We both laugh.

In the cage, I know the perfect time to shoot, to strike, and to circle, but one-on-one with a girl is like me in the ring with welterweight champion GSP. I'm overmatched and undertrained.

"OK," I repeat.

"Do you think I could come to one of your fights sometime?" she asks in small voice.

"I'll fight a few days after my eighteenth birthday, so sure," I say. The thought makes me pick up the pace a little. Despite May Li's oversized book bag and her small frame, she keeps up with me. "I'll get two tickets."

"Two?"

"One for you and one for your boyfriend."

She blushes. "Nong, I don't have a boyfriend."

"OK. So, do you—"

"I'm so busy with orchestra, school, and planning for college, I don't have time for one."

I nod and keep walking with my chin up, which is amazing considering the head kick I just took.

* * * * *

After I finish walking May Li home—talking nonstop to cover the uncomfortable silence from her—I decide to walk over to Ywj's place one block away. I want to thank Kia in person for the robe.

I'm halfway there when my phone rings. Lue. I hesitate for a second before I pick up. I know what's coming.

"Cuz, what up?" I answer.

"Hey. So, have you thought about me joining your dojo?" he says. "I want to make sure I have your blessing."

I pause. I can't discourage him or stop him from joining, so why am I fighting this? "Sure. You got a belt in tae kwon do, right? Mr. Hodge only lets in people who already have some training."

"Black, also in karate. The dojo I'm in now doesn't do MMA, and you've inspired me."

"The Ninja Warrior is an inspiration to many!"

He cracks up. "Like that, cuz, I mean, you really believe that. I remember when we used to play football, you'd always get creamed. And how your brothers used to pick on you."

"Your point?"

"My point is you're a different person when you talk about MMA. You're not that runt that Ywj always called you. You talk and act like you're the Ninja Warrior. I want that."

"I'm a fighter and philosopher." He cracks up again. "Call me Confucius Cro Cop."

"Cro Cop?"

Lue doesn't know what he's in for as I start teaching him his first MMA history lesson.

⬚ ⬚ ⬚ ⬚ ⬚ ⬚

I knock on Ywj's door. I called Kia, but it went right to voicemail. She works all the time since

Ywj lost his job.

Bao peeks through the bottom of the window. He opens the door, and I swoop him up in my arms, press him over my head, and gently lay him on the floor. He doesn't stop laughing as he calls out, "Uncle Ninja Warrior!"

"Is your mom home?" I ask.

He shakes his head. "She had to work late."

"Your dad?"

"I don't know where he is."

"You're here by yourself, Mighty Bao?" He nods and smiles, proud of himself.

I stare at his right eye, which sports an ugly bruise. "What happened to your eye?"

He gives me this funny look like he swallowed his tongue. "I'm not supposed to say."

I sigh and pull him close to me. This is not happening in my family again. They say crap runs downhill, and the littlest person is on the receiving end. I've been on the bottom of that mountain. I'm not going to allow Bao to go through what I did. "Mighty Bao, you wanna wrestle? Would you like that?" He claps loudly and runs to his room.

We play-wrestle in his room until I hear the back door open.

"Kia?" I shout and make a break for the door.

"Uncle Ninja Warrior, come on!" Bao shouts behind me. I look toward him, smile, and then turn back to the door. Kia stands there, looking tired and sweaty in her laundry uniform.

"Hey, Nong, what's up?" she asks.

"I wanted to thank you for the robe."

"I heard it didn't help."

"Well, not yet. But defeat brews the tea of victory."

She laughs.

"Kia, can I ask you something?" She nods, and I point toward the kitchen. "Mighty Bao, I'll be right back," I call out. "That's a promise and a threat."

Kia and I walk into the kitchen. She starts to pull out a chair, but I block it. "Kia, why do you let Ywj hit Bao like that? How can you let that happen?"

She doesn't look at me or speak for a few moments. Finally she says, "I guess I'm afraid."

"Of what?"

She pauses. "Everything."

"But still, Bao's your son," I plead. "You're his mother. You have to say something."

She looks up, tears in her voice and fear in her eyes. "Why? Your mom never said anything to your dad when he beat Ywj."

CHAPTER 8

"Slip your hand in like this, by his elbow." Mr. Matsuda's showing me how to escape a rear naked choke. Ever since I lost the spar fight, he and Mr. Hodge have spent more time with me, in part because I asked them to watch me until I know I can apply the hold or counter perfectly.

I take Mr. Matsuda's place on the mat with Shawn behind me. Shawn locks in the choke hold, and I tuck my chin and slip my hand in between my chin and Shawn's arm like Mr. Matsuda showed me.

"Okay, now pull down on his arm and bridge

your back!"

I do as he says. Arching back against Shawn's body while pulling down on his arm works, and I escape. Mr. Matsuda bows in respect. "Good, Nong. Now, the best way to escape is not to get caught in it!"

Shawn gets up and starts walking over toward the weight machine.

"Hey, where are you going?" I yell after him. "Get back here."

"Why?"

"I need to do it again," I say. Mr. Matsuda smiles as I fall on the mat and wait for Shawn.

* * * * * *

After working with Shawn for a half hour while Mr. Matsuda showed us other escapes, I know it's time to talk with Mr. Hodge. We didn't talk on the way back to the dojo after the fight at MMA Academy, and I've been avoiding him. I hit the speed bag while I wait for him to get a free moment.

I'm throwing hard strikes when I'm distracted. Mr. Hodge stands next to Marcus Robinson.

Marcus is the dojo's star student. He's doing one last amateur fight, and then he's turning pro.

"Nong, come here!" Mr. Hodge yells. I throw one last jab and jog across the dojo.

Mr. Hodge introduces me to Marcus and talks about Marcus's accomplishments with pride in his voice. A pride I want him to have when talking about me. Mr. Hodge then tells Marcus about my scrimmage fight. He praises me, but also makes it clear that it was my mistake that doomed me. "Nong was the better fighter, but just not that night, I guess."

"What are you again? Bantam?" Marcus asks.

"Featherweight," I answer. Although I'm sure a post-loss eating binge has me over the limit.

"Well, feather, let's see what you got," Marcus says.

"Serious?"

"You only get better facing better fighters," Marcus says.

I shake my head and smile. "How do you know you're a better fighter than me?"

He laughs. "I guess we're about to find out, right?"

I'm standing straight up, but how he says it makes my knees buckle like a KO punch.

Marcus and I drill hard over in the corner, mostly on grappling and defending against takedowns. I don't know how he can even grip me with sweat oozing out of my every pore. Every time he takes me down, he explains how I could defend against it. My neck hurts from nodding so much as I soak in everything he's showing me.

"Keep your head in the game for these drills," he warns. "Think when you're drilling, and think before you get in the cage about what you want to do," Marcus said. "But once you're inside, you need to let your trained instincts guide you."

"I did that, and I got choked out."

"No, from what I heard, you didn't get choked out—you choked."

I hang my head like it holds all 145 pounds.

"Mr. Hodge said you went in overconfident, and then when you got on the ground, you panicked. Stay calm, and you can win."

I start to argue, but Marcus shuts me down.

"Overcome the fear and you can win. I've lost before. You can't win every fight."

"I'm not afraid of losing," I whisper.

"Then what are you afraid of?"

I bounce nervously on the balls of my feet as I think. Fighting in the dojo wasn't a big deal. In public, with people watching, it felt different. Riskier. Too much like the humiliation of getting knocked around by my brothers as the runt.

Marcus shrugs, letting it go. "After practice, we'll spar for a while in the cage. We'll see what you've got, Ninja Warrior."

⸭ ⸭ ⸭ ⸭ ⸭

As I head to the shower, I run into Hector. I saw him drilling with Marcus as well. Even though Hector outweighs him by sixty pounds, just like with me, Marcus was clearly in charge.

"Good workout?" Hector asks.

"I'm just getting started," I reply. "You fighting Marcus tonight?"

"You bet."

"It will be so much fun to watch myself get pounded again. I can hardly wait."

"Nong, come on, it was just one fight."

"Easy for you to say."

"Why?" Hector asks.

"Because you won."

Before Hector says anything else, his cell rings. It's his dad. They argue as usual. It seems strange to me—I don't talk back or question my dad. I've learned what would happen. It's not a two-sided argument. It's how Ywj got lots of bruises.

CHAPTER 9

"Close the distance, Nong!" Mr. Hodge shouts.

Marcus is fast, with good defenses, but some of my leg kicks get through. I try a takedown. He sprawls and grabs the clinch. I feel his fingers lock around the back of my neck and try to get my knees up to protect myself, but he's too quick. A hard knee to the chin sends me back to the mat, and he pounces on me. In full mount, he starts throwing elbows and punches, just like the guy did the other night. Mr. Hodge blows the whistle.

It's like that whack-a-mole game; every time

I stand up, he knocks me back down. My only chance is from the mat. He takes me down and starts working an arm submission. I feel the pressure relax for a microsecond, and I pop my hips. Before I can stand, Marcus drags me back down flat on my back. But he's off balance.

I quickly move to rubber guard, getting my legs high against his back. I eat a hard elbow to the jaw as I raise my head. As he reaches in, I'm quicker and I lock my hands behind his head, threading the fingers together. When he tries to snare my left leg, I slip my right leg from behind and get it under his chin. I push up with the leg and pull down with my hands. Mr. Hodge blows the whistle before Marcus can tap or escape.

"Perfect gogoplata!" Mr. Matsuda says.

◾ ◾ ◾ ◾ ◾ ◾

Marcus and I spar for another few rounds until I'm exhausted. I never get him in another submission, but he never locks one in on me again either. He probably would have won every round but one on points. Still, it's my best fight yet.

As I'm driving home, I'm feeling pumped

up, happy, and hungry. The happiness leaves when I see the old gold Lexus in the driveway. Ywj's car. My mom's car is gone, but Dad's pickup is there. I drive around the block a few times, but each time I swing past, the Lexus remains.

I'm thinking about sleeping in the parking lot of the dojo when my cell rings. It's Dad. He tells me I'm out past my curfew and to get home. I hope Bao is there with Ywj, but I also know he shouldn't be up so late.

I park on the street, walk by the Lexus, and head inside. Dad and Ywj sit at the kitchen table, laughing and smoking, playing cards. Ywj drinks a beer, Dad sips tea. Bao isn't around.

"Sorry I'm late," I mumble as I walk as quickly as I can, head down, toward my room.

"Come say hello to your brother," Dad commands. "It's great to have Ywj home, no?"

Before I can answer, Ywj jumps up and gets me in a headlock. "Hello, runt!" he hisses. Suddenly I'm not the Ninja Warrior; I'm Nong Vang, the kid who won't fight back while his dad laughs at him.

CHAPTER 10

"Welcome to a very special edition of MTV's Bully Beatdown," *says host Jason "Mayhem" Miller. "In this edition, we'll have not one but three bullies step into the cage with our guest MMA fighter. The rules are simple: the bully starts the round with $5,000 but loses $1,000 every time he is forced to tap out. The second round is a three-minute kickboxing round. The bully wins $5,000 if he can survive the entire three minutes, but does not earn anything if he quits or gets KO'd, or if referee Big John McCarthy stops the fight.*

"So tonight, for the first time, we're set to give

away $30,000 if the Vang brothers can defeat the secret MMA fighter. For reasons that will become clear, the identity of the Vang brothers' victim has been kept secret from them. So, let's get ready for this special edition of Bully Beatdown.

"From St. Louis, please welcome the Vang brothers and see the tale of the tape."

Ywj Vang:	*age 25*	*6 feet*	*245 pounds*
Tha Vang:	*age 23*	*5 feet, 10 inches*	*215 pounds*
Vam Vang:	*age 21*	*5 feet, 9 inches*	*200 pounds*

"And now welcome our mystery MMA fighter, age 18, 5 feet, 4 inches and 145 pounds," Miller says. The crowd boos the bullies and cheers the MMA fighter, whose face remains hidden from the audience and his foes thanks to a hooded gold robe. Miller walks over to the fighter.

"So, will you start with Vam?" Miller asks, but the fighter shakes his head. "Tha?"

Again the fighter shakes his head, and then points toward the oldest and largest, Ywj Vang.

In his corner, Ywj laughs and shakes his head in agreement. The other two leave the cage.

Miller puts the microphone in front of the face of the MMA fighter. "It's now time to reveal the true identity of our mystery fighter. Please welcome UFC featherweight champion and the youngest of the Vang brothers, Nong 'Ninja Warrior' Vang." Nong tosses his head back and the hood falls off. His two brothers outside the cage look concerned, but Ywj shows no emotion as he and his youngest brother go to the center of the cage and listen to the instructions. Nong refuses to look his brother in the eye but nods his head as McCarthy explains the rules of the first round. "No strikes of any kind, only grappling and submissions."

Ywj pulls up his sagging sweatpants as he returns to his side of the cage. Nong doesn't leave the center of the cage. When the bell rings, he assumes his fighting pose. Ywj laughs and then charges at his younger brother, but Nong executes a sweeping hip throw, putting his brother on the mat with a thud. Before Ywj can scramble to his feet, Nong gets position beside him. Using his near arm, Nong encircles his brother's head in a headlock and then grabs Ywj's wrist, bending the arm upwards. Nong quickly maneuvers his arm through the "hole" created by Ywj's bent wrist, then locks his own wrist. Nong barely starts to crank when Ywj taps from the pressure. "Our first tap out via the Anaconda vise," Miller says.

Nong and Ywj regain their feet. Ywj tries to snatch Nong's head, but Nong tosses his brother to the mat with a double leg. Almost before Ywj lands, Nong's on top and repeats the Anaconda vise. Tap.

Ywj is slow in getting to his feet and circles for a long time before he tries to take Nong down again. He shoots in, but in doing so, Ywj ducks his head. Nong wraps his right arm under Ywj's neck. With his left hand, Nong grasps his right hand. With the choke locked in, Nong wraps his legs around Ywj's body. Ywj taps almost immediately.

Once more, Ywj tries to shoot, but Nong sprawls and locks in another guillotine choke, this time from his knees. Nong falls back, wrapping his legs around Ywj's body. Ywj once again submits, the fourth time in less than a minute. Ywj gets to his feet, cursing under his breath, but Nong stays on the mat, daring his brother to take the fight to the floor. When Ywj gets close, Nong grabs his ankle, bringing his brother down. As Ywj leans in again, Nong wraps his right leg around the back of his brother's neck. With his left leg, he pins Ywj's arm. "Triangle choke!" Miller shouts as Ywj taps for final time.

Ywj talks with his brothers before the kickboxing round as he's fitted with gloves, shin pads, and a helmet. When the bell rings, Ywj races toward Nong, throwing wild punches that don't connect. Nong answers with a kick right on his brother's knee. Ywj crumbles to the mat. McCarthy counts to eight before Ywj stands awkwardly. He can barely move and has no power in his punches.

Nong continues to punish Ywj with jabs and hooks until Ywj's face is a flood of sweat. A liver kick connects, and Ywj stumbles toward the mat. But before he lands, Nong greets him with a head kick, and Ywj is lights-out. As the audience cheers, Nong stares at his two other brothers and then motions for them to come into the cage. The brothers look at Nong, down at Ywj, back at Nong, and then for the nearest exit sign.

Nong removes his mouthpiece, stands over his fallen big brother, and shouts, "Who is the runt now?" Scanning the crowd, Nong points at an older man and laughs until his sides hurt.

CHAPTER 11

"Happy birthday, runt!" Ywj says, then slaps my back hard with his left hand. His right hand carries a full plate of crab legs from the buffet. We're celebrating my birthday with dinner at Grand City Buffet, my dad's and my older brothers' favorite Chinese restaurant. Since they don't need to worry about making weight, this is a feast for them. For me, it's torture.

I mumble something and take a bite from my veggie-filled plate. In front of me is a pile of gifts and envelopes from my family. In my car, I have the same from people at the dojo.

"Hey, Bao, you some kind of rock star?" Lue asks Bao, who's wearing sunglasses indoors.

"He's got an eye infection," Ywj answers for Bao as he wraps his arms around his son. "You know little kids. They're all bacteria-filled runts."

Bao doesn't react to the insult, which means he's used to it. When I first started at the dojo and felt real strikes for the first time, I thought I'd forever be in pain. But you learn to absorb the blows.

"Open our birthday card first!" Dad says between bites of chicken wings.

Mom points it out, and I reach for it. She's all smiles.

I open the gold envelope and pull out the fancy card. Inside it is a check for eighteen hundred dollars, except it's not made out to me. The payee is Kirkwood Community College.

"Nong, you've made us so proud doing so well in school," Mom says. Dad nods in agreement and then takes a chicken wing off Mom's plate. "So your father wants you to continue your education in the fall, maybe even start taking classes this summer."

"Thanks, Mom, but I don't want to go to college. I want to train and fight full-time."

Dad laughs. "Nong, get serious. We've supported this MMA thing while you're in school since it keeps you out of trouble, but now it's time to think about your future. You need a real plan."

"I am serious," I counter.

Dad frowns. "Son, your brothers and I have done fine even though we didn't go to college. But as my youngest son, I want you to live the American dream, and that means college."

"Wait a minute," Ywj says. "Maybe he could be a pro wrestler. Remember how they used to have midget wrestling?" Everybody laughs but me, Mom, Kia, and Lue.

"But college isn't *my* dream, Dad. I want to be a fighter and—"

"It's decided," he says and then goes back to eating food off his and Mom's plates. I open up the other presents. The ones from my brothers are all the same: DVDs of seasons of *The Ultimate Fighter*. I already own them, but it's not like they would ask or pay attention.

"Open mine next," Lue says and then hands me his present. It's heavy.

I rip open the paper. Inside is a huge book. *The UFC Encyclopedia.* "Thanks, Lue!"

"One day, cuz, we'll both be in there!"

Vam laughs. "Yeah, Nong 'The Runt' Vang, I can see it!"

My face flushes as red as the sweet and sour pork on Lue's plate.

"Shut up, Vam," Lue says.

"Make me!" Vam pushes his chair back, suddenly serious. Lue does the same. They stand nose to nose.

"Sit down, the both of you," Dad says. Vam obeys, and after a few seconds, so does Lue. When they sit, I stand. Even standing, I'm only a little taller than my brothers are sitting down.

"I need to make a call," I say quickly and even more quickly head for the door. Once outside in the parking lot, I walk past the smokers and get in my car. Before I pull out my phone, I take out the birthday card that May Li gave me. I dial the number and take a deep breath.

"Hey, May Li, I wanted to thank you for the card," I say.

"Happy birthday! I can't believe you're eighteen. Do you feel different?"

It's like I can still hear the laughter from inside and feel Ywj's hard slap on the back.

"Nong?" May Li is still waiting for my response.

"I don't think I'll feel different until I have my first amateur fight next Friday," I say. "You said that you'd like to come watch, a while ago. Still want me to get you a ticket?" I tense up waiting for an answer.

"I'd love to, but the senior recital is that night."

"Oh. OK," I say.

"No, Nong, KO."

I laugh. I tell her more about my fight, and she tells me about her recital. The more we talk, the more comfortable it feels.

"It's a lot of pressure we're both under," she says. "Sometimes I think the pressure is worse than the concert itself. I just can't stand not to do well. It makes me feel like such a loser."

"May Li, you're the smartest person I know. How could you feel like a loser?"

"I don't know, I've always been this way. Aren't you afraid of failing? Losing your fight?"

I pause, startled by how much we have in common. It's not losing I'm afraid of—it's people thinking I'm a loser. But I can't say that. "I'm not going to lose."

"Well then, I'm sorry I can't be there to see you win," she says.

Before I can respond, I hear Bao crying outside. Ywj drags him toward his car with Kia two steps behind. And I know my moment of truth isn't just in the cage in ten days, it's right in front of me, right now. I wrap up with May Li, get out of the car, and walk chin up under a dark Missouri sky. Kia and Bao are in the Lexus. Ywj stands in front of it, talking on his phone and smoking.

"Ywj, I want to talk to you," I say.

"I'm busy," he mutters, then goes back to his call. I grab the phone from his hand.

"What are you doing, little man?"

I bounce on the balls of my feet like I'm in

the cage, setting up a strike. "Listen to me. I won't stand for it. You won't hit Bao again or call him a runt. Do you understand?"

"Nong, this is none of your business."

I notice he doesn't deny it. "It is my business. He's my nephew."

"He's my son."

"Then treat him like one."

He pulls in a drag from his smoke. "I'm treating him like Dad treated me."

"It's still not right."

"What are you going do about it?" He stares me down, and in only a few seconds, I blink, losing the faceoff.

I hand Ywj his phone and walk away. I hope he didn't notice my hand shaking when he took the phone. There is a moment of truth coming, but not here, not now, not yet.

c c c c c

Back inside the restaurant, my other two brothers are still eating crab legs and laughing. Dad beams with pride at his big, strapping sons, like size makes you a man or something. I pick up

Lue's present and sit down next him. We flip through the book together.

"Check out the moves these guys were famous for," he says. "It's crazy."

"Yeah. But . . . you can learn most all of it at Mr. Hodge's dojo. That is, if you still want to join."

"Really?"

I nod and then we fist-bump. "One day we'll tap gloves in the ring, and then you'll tap to the Ninja Warrior!" I say.

Lue laughs. "We'll see about that. I outweigh you by, like, twenty pounds."

"Won't make any difference because inside that cage, I'm a different person. Here you know me as Nong Vang, but in the cage, I'm the Ninja Warrior."

⌐ ⌐ ⌐ ⌐ ⌐

Back home, I head up to my room. I toss and turn as the two sides of me battle for control. The confident Ninja Warrior shoots on the insecure runt Nong Vang, but Nong always seems to win, especially tonight.

Since I can't sleep, I turn on the computer and start watching fights. But I just keep focusing on the look on the loser's face. I pause the DVD and head for my closet. I pull out a grocery bag from behind a pile of blankets, emptying my stash of candy bars and chips onto the bed. Ripping open the bag of chips feels like ripping open my presents. But then I think about what my dad said about my future, and all the nasty things Ywj and my other brothers have said about me in the past. Nobody believes in me as a fighter, and right now, that includes me.

CHAPTER 12

Hector and I have our first amateur fights on the same night, so I give him a ride. But this time, we are both silent on the drive to the arena. I'm too nervous even to talk too much. When we arrive, the parking lot is still pretty empty. I park, and we walk toward the building.

"Where you going?" He's headed for the front door. I point him toward the back.

Hector grunts like he's afraid to waste energy on talking. We find a back door labeled "Fighters' Entrance" and head inside. We spot Mr. Hodge and Marcus in the locker room.

"Nong, Hector—listen." Mr. Hodge begins to explain how the weigh-ins will work. Hector keeps nodding. I don't move a muscle until we all leave the locker room for the arena area.

Marcus, as a flyweight, gets called first. Just looking at him compared to his opponent, it's obvious Marcus is going to win. From the look in his foe's eyes, he knows that too. It's like they don't need to wait the hour before the fight to start—it could be declared over right now.

When they call featherweight, I take a deep breath and walk toward the scale with purpose. The other featherweight weighs in first. Right on the money at 145. I take off everything except my briefs and prepare to mount the scale, but first I stare down the other fighter like Jackson taught me. He doesn't look like a winner— there is no way I will lose.

"148," the judge says. I look at the scale, and he's not joking. I'm three pounds over the limit. I keep looking anywhere except at Mr. Hodge. I put my clothes back on, bow my head in humiliation, and start toward the locker room.

"Where are you going?" Mr. Hodge asks.

"Back to the locker room," I answer.

"The locker room is for fighters, and you're not fighting tonight," Mr. Hodge says and points toward the arena. "Sit in the hard chairs with the civilians."

I walk out into the empty arena. I close my eyes and try to visualize being in Vegas, with thousands in attendance, or at a stadium show in Brazil. But the images won't come, like I've lost the ability to dream.

With nothing to do but wait, I call home to tell Mom not to bother to come to the fight. She blames herself for my not making weight, saying she should have supported me more, but I don't let her beat up on herself. I tell her I own this and I'll suffer the consequences.

"What do you think Mr. Hodge will do?" she asks.

"I don't know and I don't care."

"Are you quitting?"

"No, the opposite," I say. "I'll work harder. Then, when I do step in the cage for the first time, I'll know for sure that I'll win."

"Is there anything I can do?"

I pause. I want to tell her yes, I want you to find a time machine, go back in time, and step in when Dad hit Ywj. Then tell Dad he shouldn't let Ywj beat up Tha, who beat up Vam, who beat me up with the others.

I watch as the crew sets up the cage. I close my eyes and see myself in the cage. Not the Ninja Warrior, but just Nong Vang.

"Nong, are you there?" Mom asks.

"Not yet."

CHAPTER 13

"You're not coming in with me?" Lue asks through my open Honda window. We're in an empty lot across from the Missouri MMA dojo, also known as Nong's House of Shame.

"I'm not ready to face Mr. Hodge and Mr. Matsuda yet," I confess.

"Look, there are worse things in the world than not making weight," Lue says.

I nod in agreement. Fighting, losing, and being humiliated would have been worse. I chose the lesser of two evils. "Besides, if I come back, I'll come back to the adult class."

"But I thought we could train together," Lue says. "Ninja Warrior and Lightning Lue."

"No, just being Lue Vang will do," I say. "Besides, family and fighting shouldn't mix."

"Man, that's too bad." Lue says. "I thought at your graduation party in a couple of weeks, we could spar, show off the sport for the whole family. You'd probably win, but it'd be fun."

"I don't think most people think it's a sport," I say. "Just 'cause we're not on an actual team."

"You guys don't consider yourself a team?"

I think about Hector, Jackson, and Meghan and realize that I'd lied to Lue. Not just about why I didn't make weight—blaming it on a broken scale at home—but about fighting and family not mixing. "No, my dojo mates aren't teammates. In some ways, they're more like a family."

"Well, I guess families and fighting do mix sometimes." He smiles and waves good-bye and heads into the dojo.

I'm barely settled when my phone rings. It's Jackson. This makes the fifth time he's called in the past week, since my shame. That's two times less than Hector. Meghan has texted a couple of times.

To kill time before giving Lue a ride back home, I play games and watch fights on my phone. Ywj is at my folks' house again, so I can't go there. I'd go see Kia and Bao, but that just makes me mad: first at Ywj, then at myself, and then back at Ywj. And of course at my dad. I brood and think while I wait.

After a long two hours, Lue calls and I turn the car on. I look across the way, and I don't see Hector. After winning his first fight, he probably graduated to the adult class. Jackson comes out, talking with Meghan. He walks toward the bus stop, while Meghan stays behind and talks with Mr. Hodge.

Lue climbs into the car and can't stop talking about the class, including how Jackson knocked out one of the other new students. "But everybody is asking about you," he says.

"Not talking trash about me?" I mutter.

"Okay, a little. They say you're ready for UFC, at least in terms of trash-talking."

I laugh. "Well, if I could fight with my

mouth, I'd do better."

Lue sinks into the passenger seat. "Word going around is someone knows why you didn't make weight. They said you did it on purpose. They said it was because you were scared."

"That's a lie," I lie. "Who said that? I'll teach that punk kid a lesson."

He looks out the window as he says, "It was Mr. Hodge."

⬠ ⬠ ⬠ ⬠ ⬠ ⬠

After I drop Lue off, I drive back to the dojo. Mr. Hodge's car is gone, so I head back home. Then I notice Meghan biking on the side of the road. I get ahead of her and pull off to the shoulder. She slows down at the sight, I hope, of my familiar beat-up green Honda.

I get out of the car. "Meghan, hey!"

She stops her bike, takes off her helmet, and lets her long hair fly in the wind. "Clark Kent, what are you doing out here? Are you the Ninja Stalker now?"

I laugh. "Hey, can we talk?"

There's a puzzled look on her face. In the

two years I've known her, I know I've never said those four words to her. Or her to me. "There's a Starbucks up the road," she says. "Meet me there."

I climb back in the car and drive slowly to the Starbucks. I park, go inside, wait, and prepare my game plan.

After she locks her bike, she comes in. "You want anything, Clark?" she asks from the counter. I think of all the ways I could answer that question.

"See if they got any fat-burning teas," I finally say.

She laughs, orders a flavored latte for herself, and comes over to the table with it. "This is weird," she says as she sits down. "Have we ever had coffee before?"

"Doubt it," I answer. I don't tell her one of the reasons is that I had a crush on her at one point—probably like every other guy at the dojo—but fighting was more important to me than flirting. Mr. Hodge has a hard rule about the girls and guys in his dojo not dating.

"So talk," she says.

"I heard Mr. Hodge said that I didn't make weight because I was afraid. Is that true?"

She sips the drink like she's stalling. She takes two more sips and then finally answers quietly. "Yes."

"Meghan, can I trust you?" I ask.

Again, the puzzled look, followed by a sip and then an affirming nod of her head.

"You don't talk about yourself much, about your family or anything except the dojo and MMA. And I don't either, so I guess we have something in common," I begin.

"Maybe, Clark, it's because my life outside of the dojo is so dull."

"No, I think because your life outside of the dojo is different than inside, right?

Another affirming head nod.

"So, maybe you'll understand what I'm talking about," I say, and then I start in. Unlike one of my UFC information dumps, this isn't blathering to show off. Unlike my trash-talking, this isn't flapping my gums to cover up nervousness, but the opposite. I tell her about the fear of getting humiliated and where that comes from. I tell her about my brothers, and even about Bao. I even tell her about having a crush on her, and my crush on May Li. The whole time she says hardly anything. Mostly she just nods her head like Mr. Hodge does when we're drilling, to show that he's paying attention. I end with, "So what do I do?"

She focuses on her latte. "Sounds like you're battling a whole bunch of fighters at once."

"Yeah, but what do you do then?"

She sips her coffee, smiles at me, and says, "Take out the biggest one first."

I recall my *Bully Beatdown* fantasy, and I know she's right. "Do you think I can come back to the dojo?" I ask and then brace for the blow. "Do you think Mr. Hodge would let me?"

"He respects honesty more than anything else. Be honest with him, ask for another chance to show the Ninja Warrior is ready, and I'm sure he'd welcome you back. But you should come to the adult class. I'm going, and so are Jackson and that tough new fish, Tyresha."

"The Ninja Warrior's not coming back to the dojo," I say. "But Nong Vang is."

CHAPTER 14

"So that's it," I say and then let out a deep breath. Sitting in Mr. Hodge's office, I've just finished talking about what happened before my first fight—or what was supposed to be my first fight. I've told him about reaching my limit with Ywj and Bao. He hasn't reacted much, just looked as if he knew what I would say. "I'd like to come back to the dojo," I finish, meeting his eyes. My body's enjoyed the pain-free two weeks, but the fighter in me wants to live again.

"Will this happen again?" is his matter-of-fact question.

"No, I promise. If I don't make weight for my next fight, I'll quit."

He nods. "Everybody makes mistakes. It's not just a matter of not doing something again. You need to understand why you messed up in the first place. What are you going to do differently?"

"I'm going to get real," I say. "Stop trying to be great and talk tough. Stop acting like somebody I'm not. Just take what I've learned, let my instincts take over, and fight the best fight I can."

"Then let's get to work." Mr. Hodge pats me on the back and points to the dojo.

⬚ ⬚ ⬚ ⬚ ⬚ ⬚

Mr. Matsuda is not as forgiving. He makes me into a throw toy in takedown practice for all the new fighters, including Lue. Each time I hit the mat, I bounce back up, bow to Mr. Matsuda, and get ready for the next takedown. "You had enough, fatboy?" he hisses.

Being called fatboy isn't better than being called a runt, but I let it bounce off. "No, sir."

"Sweeping hip throws, let's go!" Mr. Matsuda demonstrates the move on me with too much zeal and then has everyone use it on me twice. Everybody does it well except for Lue, who has trouble keeping his balance. Matsuda shakes his head and mumbles, "new fish," as he walks away.

"Here, Lue, let me show you," I say. "Tyresha, would you mind?"

Tyresha, a tough girl with a wrestling background, locks up with me. Rather than just showing them the move, I talk them through it. For Lue, I show him how and where to plant his feet, set his hips, and balance himself as he executes the move.

"Okay, Lue, you try again." Lue and I lock up, and I let him take me down. This time he keeps his balance and executes the move perfectly. The other students applaud. "Good job, Lue."

Lue adds his applause. "No—good job, Nong."

"Welcome back, Clark!" I hear. I turn around to see Meghan applauding as well. "You talk to Mr. Hodge?"

"I did exactly what you said."

"Are you coming to adult class?"

"Yes, but I also want to stay with the teen classes now that school is almost over."

"Now, don't be a bully to them, Clark."

"Trust me, that's one thing I'll never be."

□ □ □ □ □ □

Mr. Hodge spends most of the class in his office. Mr. Matsuda works with other students and leaves me in charge of Lue and other new students. With about a half hour left in the class, Mr. Hodge emerges from his office. He's got a rare expression on his face: a smile.

"Everybody, over here!" Drills stop immediately and students come to the center.

"I just got off the phone with the fight promoter," Mr. Hodge says. "He had a scratch for this Friday, and it happens to be in the featherweight division. So, Nong, you'll get another chance in a few days. You ready?"

"I am." I'll graduate on Thursday, and then fight on Friday. Every exit is also an entrance ramp.

Mr. Hodge points at Lue. "Let's get him ready. Two three-minute rounds, full contact."

Lue and I put on our equipment and head into the cage. We touch gloves and start the spar. Lue's strikes aren't much, but he's got good footwork. Given that and his size, he'll be hard to take down. With his tae kwon do background, he'll be strong on kicks.

"Close the distance, Nong!" Mr. Hodge shouts. I follow instructions and get in close. Lue tries some judo throws, but that's his mistake. I'm quicker, and I get position and double-leg him to the mat. I get side control, but he's too big and strong for me to move. I let him up, circle, and take him down again, this time with a single leg. On the mat it's more of the same.

"Lue, you've got to defend. Go on the offensive!" Mr. Matsuda shouts.

Lue throws a few tentative kicks, and I rush in with a flurry of solid strikes. Nothing fancy, just hard right jabs, overhand lefts, and strong front kicks. The round ends with my fingers locked around his neck in the clinch, and him defending against knee strikes.

Mr. Hodge walks over to my corner. He says nothing, just pats my shoulder again as I stay loose.

The whistle blows, and Lue goes on offense, mainly with kicks that don't land. I throw a hard front kick to his knee that connects. When his knee buckles, he drops his head. I fight through a weak jab and get my arm wrapped tight around his neck, increasing the pressure on the standing guillotine choke by locking my legs around his body. He taps immediately.

Lue and I touch gloves. He takes out his mouthpiece. "I told you. You're way better."

I take out my mouthpiece and hug Lue. "Maybe now, but you'll improve over time.

"Helps to have a good teacher." He bows to me, and I return the gesture.

I look over the students in the dojo, so eager and excited. "Who is next?" I ask.

Before anyone volunteers, I point at Jackson, who stands in the back row. At six feet and over 200 pounds, he's the fighter who most resembles Ywj. He steps forward and scowls; it's what he does. "You're sure you don't want to pick on someone your own size, Ninja Warrior?"

"I'm Nong, not Ninja, but let's get it on!" I shout at Jackson, but I think about Ywj. I bang my gloves and motion him into the cage. I know I can win a fair fight, but most fights in life aren't fair. Still, even if there isn't always fairness in the world, that doesn't mean there can't be justice.

CHAPTER 15

"Congratulations, Nong!" Mom says as she hugs me under the big "happy graduation" banner hanging in our backyard. It's a pretty noisy party because most of my family is here.

"Well done, son!" Dad adds. Kia takes a picture of Mom, Dad, and me together. Dad actually seems proud of me for doing something, but maybe because it's something that he wanted me to achieve. I wonder if he'll be as proud when—I mean if—I win my first fight.

Because of my fight tomorrow night, I have to pass up all the food Mom and others prepared. I've weighed in at 140 every morning and I've thrown away my junk food stash. I will make weight, I will fight, and I will win, but if I don't, it doesn't make me a loser.

"Thanks for the invite," Jackson says, and we bump fists. Tyresha stands next to him. I look for May Li so I can stand next to her.

"Nong, lots of pressure to keep up the winning streak now," Tyresha says. Both Hector and Jackson won their debut fights. Meghan fights her first amateur bout tomorrow night as well.

I shrug. "Yeah, I'm not worried about that. I just want to fight a smart fight," I respond. Jackson, Tyresha, and I talk MMA until May Li comes over. She's with one of her good friends, Charlotte. Here it is: my worlds colliding. I make introductions, and they seem to mix pretty well for two groups of people that have nothing in common except me.

"So, May Li, they gave me two free tickets to the fight. Would you like them?" I ask. It's a calculated risk that she is less likely to reject me in public than in private.

May Li looks at Charlotte, then back at me, and says, "You won't get hurt, will you?"

"Probably, but that's part of the sport," I answer. "It's part of life." I give her the tickets.

"Amen," Jackson says, which for some reason makes Tyresha laugh. The five of us talk about school, graduating, and our plans. May Li and Charlotte are going away to colleges in California. The only thing that Jackson, Tyresha, and I know for sure is we're going to continue to train for MMA, although Tyresha says she's thinking about switching dojos. I don't ask why, but I couldn't imagine better teachers than Mr. Hodge and Mr. Matsuda.

"Hey, new fish!" Jackson says when Lue joins our group. Lue's girlfriend, Cindy, stands by his side. Lue and Tyresha talk about how hard training at the dojo is, while Jackson and I tell stories about when we started. "You listen, you learn. You talk, you get beat, understand?"

Lue nods his head and asks more questions about the training. Jackson talks about how the training doesn't build just MMA skills but confidence in yourself as a person too. May Li and

Charlotte seem interested and compare their high-pressure school careers with what we went through in the dojo. My separate worlds seem not so different after all.

Then Ywj shows up. He slaps me on the back, hard. "These your fighter buds, runt?" he asks.

"Runt?" Jackson asks. I take a deep breath and let it pass. Not now, not yet.

Tha and Vam come up behind us like two dark clouds. Except for Jackson, who is as tall as Ywj, the three of them tower over us. I introduce my brothers to everyone.

"This runt thinks he's a fighter, but all I remember about him is Tha and Vam kicking his scrawny butt all the time," Ywj says and laughs way too loud. I notice that when he laughs, he sounds and looks just like my dad. "You're sure MMA isn't fake like WWE?"

I look at Jackson and shake my head. "Let it go," I whisper. It's best to let these dark clouds pass. After another Nong humiliation story, my brothers head over to the food area.

"What jerks," Tyresha says. "Why do you

put up with that?"

"Because I always have," is my weak answer.

"My sisters used to tease me by calling me fat, stupid, and ugly," May Li says.

"I'd like to meet your sisters sometime," I say, "so I could tell them how wrong they are."

My awkward flattery creates a low buzz and a wave of giggles. But the laughter in our group is soon overwhelmed by the sound of Bao crying. I stare at Ywj, Kia, and Bao. It looks like Bao just knocked over a plate of food. Kia's cleaning it up while Ywj yells at Bao. "He spilled it, he'll clean it up. You stupid runt!"

When Bao hesitates, Ywj pulls his arm hard and sends him to the ground.

I decide that's it. Here. Now.

"Ywj, leave him alone!" I shout from across the yard.

Ywj looks at me, as does most everyone else. Pretty soon, the noisy party turns quiet as I walk toward my older brother. My mom takes a step toward me, but Dad pulls her back.

"I told you, runt, this isn't any of your business."

"This isn't about Bao, it's about me. I'm going to do something you never did for me."

"What?"

"Make it a fair fight."

"Fight? You want to fight me, runt? I don't think so." Ywj's laughing, and so are Tha and Vam. If Jackson could see the hard scowl on my face, he'd be proud. But my back is to my friends and my eyes are on my family. Dad's got the oddest look I can't describe on his face.

I'm so close Ywj is casting a shadow over me in the twilight sun.

"I'm not going to beat you up at your graduation party," Ywj says over Bao's crying.

"You're not going to beat me up. You're not going to touch Bao ever again," I respond.

Ywj looks over at Dad for a cue. But Dad doesn't say anything or get involved. Why should he start now? "Easy," Ywj finally replies. "I don't want you to get hurt." Ywj reminds me of the Ninja Warrior, somebody who talks tough but fights weak or not at all.

"Come on—Kia, Bao, we're leaving," Ywj says. When Bao runs toward me, Ywj grabs his arm and Bao screams in pain. Ywj lets go of Bao when my right foot connects with his head.

Ywj staggers for a second and then rushes toward me. Like most bullies, he doesn't know how to fight from in front, just behind. I deliver a solid front kick to his left knee. I keep throwing kicks at his knees and thighs, chopping him down like a tall tree. Soon, he'll be my size.

Mom screams for us to stop. So does Kia. For both, it's too little and way too late.

"You kick like a girl!" Ywj says, throwing a weak jab. I sidestep it and respond with a right jab, overhand left, and a right hook into his ribs. I think I hear a cracking sound: his ribs or my hand.

Ywj tries fighting back, but his punches miss. In close, I throw another hard front kick to his left, then right knee. When I throw a kick to his ribs, he grabs my leg. As I tumble toward the grass, I pull him down with me. He falls wildly, while I get position. A full mount.

"Knock it off!" Tha shouts and starts toward me with Vam by his side.

"I don't think so," Lue says, Jackson by his side. Vam and Tha take a step back.

Ywj's trying to get up, but he's not going anywhere as I sit on his chest. With my right hand, I throw a hard punch to the side of his head. I hear the cracking sound again. As his arms flail, I use elbow strikes, which open cuts above both his eyes. I wonder if there are tears mixing with the blood. I move from mount to side control and quickly get his back. I scissor his lower body with my legs and wrap my arms around his neck and head.

"Who is the runt now?" I whisper into Ywj's ear like a lullaby as he drifts off to sleep.

"Nong, please stop," I hear a voice say. A female voice. May Li's voice, so I stop.

⬚ ⬚ ⬚ ⬚ ⬚ ⬚

I don't go with the rest of my family to the hospital, even though I should. In the bathroom, I examine my right hand where at least two, maybe three fingers feel broken. The hand itself is bruised. I swallow some aspirin, wrap up the hand with athletic tape, and head toward my bed. Three things will happen tomorrow. First, I will fight for the first time in a real MMA competition even though I have a broken hand. Second, having stood up for myself—and for Bao—I'll see if that overdue action breaks our family apart or makes it stronger somehow. Even if my family isn't stronger, I know I am. Third, I'll see if Nong Vang can fight better in reality than Nong "Ninja Warrior" Vang ever did in his imagination.

CHAPTER 16
TALE OF THE TAPE FOR FRIDAY NIGHT FIGHTS

	NONG VANG	REG HANSON
AGE	18	25
HEIGHT	5' 4"	5' 7"
REACH	66"	71"
RECORD	0-0	7-1

CHAPTER 17

I concentrate on the ref's instructions, anything so I don't focus on the pain in my right hand. Mr. Hodge didn't ask me why I arrived at the arena with my hands already taped, nor did he ask why I cut to 140 pounds, as much as five pounds less than a featherweight opponent. The only thing he asked was if I remembered the game plan. I said I did, but told him with the reach advantage that Hanson had on me, I'd probably need to close the distance using kicks rather than punches.

After the instructions, I put out my left

glove and Hanson taps it. As I return to my corner, I want to look into the audience to see if May Li and Charlotte are there. But maybe by balancing the scales of the past, I ruined a chance of a future with May Li. I know Mom and Dad are in the audience; I know that Vam and Tha are not. I know that Ywj is still in the hospital and that I will be, after this fight. And I know that I'll do my best, because nothing's better than that.

The bell rings, and I get position in the center of the cage. Hanson tries to shoot right away, but I sidestep and throw a front kick followed by an inside leg kick. Hanson fights back with jabs. I throw a left hook that misses, but a right jab that I land hurts me more than it does him. A roundhouse kick of his connects hard with my shoulder. Knowing my fists need a break, I use every kick I know: inside roundhouse kick to his thigh, front kick to his knee, and a side kick that just misses under his chin. As long as I keep kicking, he can't focus on the offensive.

"Thirty seconds, Reg, let's go!" I hear his coach shout.

"Jab, Nong, jab!" Mr. Hodge yells.

I throw a front kick, but Hanson dodges it and hits a perfect sweeping hip throw, then follows me down and gets position behind. I sense the rear naked choke but defend it just as Mr. Matsuda taught me, by pulling down on the elbow and bridging back. I break free just as the bell rings.

In the corner, Mr. Hodge tells me I need to throw more punches, which will set up better kicks. He's right, except I can't tell him that I broke my hand before the fight, so there's only one way I'm going to win: a head kick.

When the bell rings for the second round, we circle for a long time, both tentative. I need to close the distance. I hit a strong side kick and push toward him. Up against the cage, I grab a Thai clinch and try to bring up knees, but he's too tall for me to connect to his jaw. I push away, and with distance between us, I fake a kick and a left. Then I deliver a hard right jab that connects against the little bit of flesh the helmet exposes. Hanson grunts and I wince. My attempt at a sweeping hip throw fails when he muscles me down to the mat. In my closed guard, he starts throwing quick hammer fists.

"Ten seconds!"

I pop my hips and try to regain my feet, but he pulls me down again and is back on top when the bell rings.

"Nong, why aren't you throwing jabs?" Mr. Hodge asks.

"I think I broke my hand."

"Do you want to quit?"

"No way, I want to finish this fight."

Mr. Hodge wipes the sweat off my face. "Then you need to submit him. Those first two rounds were close, but you've got to stop those takedowns. You can do this, Nong, I know it."

I put my mouthpiece back in just before the bell rings. Hanson and I touch gloves. After I land a hard roundhouse kick to his knee, he shoots and grabs a double leg. I try to push free, but it's locked and we're headed toward the mat. He lands a few punches that sting. The last one goes right to the bridge of my nose. His balance seems off, so I slip out my right leg. I get my shin under his throat and pull down with my hands locked around his neck, but with my injured hand, I can't maintain the necessary grip to execute the gogoplata. He gets free, and we're back on our feet.

"Ten seconds!"

Hanson backs away, but I rush toward him. He throws a hard shot to the body, leaving his head wide open. I throw a high roundhouse kick that lands hard. It knocks him back into the cage. I try one more, but he deflects it as the bell sounds.

We touch gloves, stand in the middle of the ring, and await the verdict from the judges. Our heads are down, but in seconds, someone will hold their head high in victory.

When I hear the announcer speak, my heart is beating faster than it was in the ring. One judge gives the match to me; another gives it to Hanson. And then it comes, harder than a head kick.

"Your winner by split decision," the announcer says, "Reg Hanson!" The two of us go through the bout ending rituals. Some people boo the decision, but not me. I know if I would have been at one hundred percent, I would probably have won, but it doesn't matter. You can't go back, you can only look forward. As I walk with Mr. Hodge back to the dressing room, I see May Li standing next to Charlotte. When May Li blows me a kiss, I wonder if I'm daydreaming. But this time, it's real.

CHAPTER 18

"How are you feeling?" Lue asks. We're on the porch of my house. Cindy stands on one side, May Li on the other. I'm just home from the hospital. Turns out my hand didn't break, but I did break two fingers.

"I'll be better when I can get back to the dojo."

"You sure do love to fight," May Li says.

"No, it's what I do," I say. "MMA is my symphony."

"Well what about your brother?" she asks. This is the first time we've talked since my graduation party. Just like with Meghan, I decide to tell her everything, even with the audience.

I end by saying, "You see, that wasn't a fight—it was payback."

"But it doesn't change the past," she says. "It's not like I can go back and stop my sisters from making fun of me. If you think this makes everything better, Nong, it doesn't."

"This wasn't just about the past," I say. "It was about Bao's future. Somebody had to protect him. Nobody stepped in to protect me. I wasn't going to let the past repeat itself with Bao."

"Why you?" Lue asks.

"Because I am the Ninja Warrior!" I say, and people laugh. I said the wrong thing, though—I should have said, because I *was* the Ninja Warrior.

 ᴄ ᴄ ᴄ ᴄ ᴄ

When I sit down for Saturday dinner with my parents, we talk about my amateur fight. If we don't talk about the fight with Ywj, then it's like it never happened. If it never happened, then we don't need to talk about the reason for the fight. If we don't talk about the reason, then Mom and Dad don't have to admit it was wrong to let Ywj bully Tha, who bullied Vam, who all bullied me.

"How did you know when to try for a submission hold?" Dad asks.

"All those hours of training at the dojo," I explain. "And good coaches."

Dad keeps asking questions, which is not something he normally does, and he seems really interested in my answers. Mom plays along, but mostly she lets Dad talk. Per usual.

"So, do you think that's what you want to do?" Mom says. Dad frowns at her.

"I can always go to college, maybe part-time, but yes, this is what I want."

My parents look at each other, their eyes moving but their mouths dormant. Dad lights up a smoke and leans back in his chair like some king on a throne. "OK," he says.

"KO," I mumble, amazed, and then ask to be excused from the table.

"Where are you going?" Mom asks.

"On a date with May Li."

"The girl that used to tutor you?" Mom asks.

"Yeah. I think I still have a lot to learn," I say with a smile.

I'm only upstairs a few minutes before Dad calls for me to come back into the kitchen. When I arrive, Kia and Bao stand there. They've both been crying.

"We're going back to St. Paul," Kia says and holds Bao closer.

"Is Ywj going with you?" Mom asks.

A loud silence overtakes the room. Kia pulls Bao closer to her and shakes her head no.

"I'll miss you, Uncle Ninja Warrior," Bao says, racing toward me.

"If you leave, Mighty Bao, then who will wrestle with me?" I ask everyone.

"Maybe May Li," Dad says, laughing. *In my dreams*, I think, *in my dreams.*

I bend down so Bao and I are the same size as he whispers, "Thank you, Uncle Ninja Warrior." I don't correct him as I hug him good-bye.

CHAPTER 19

"No, Lue, do it like this," I say and then show, as best as I can with two broken fingers, how to escape a rear naked choke. "Do you understand?"

"I think so," he answers.

"Not good enough to think, you have to know it," I say. I'm speaking to him, but also to other students in the teen class. Since I can't train, Mr. Hodge and Mr. Matsuda asked me if I could help with their summer classes, when they have more students. "You have to learn all of these holds and counter holds so they become instinct. Do you understand?"

There's lots of head nodding from the new fish.

"Okay, let's do a takedown drill." The students pair up and I give them instructions. I yell start, and they begin to practice takedowns and counters to takedown. I circle the students and give some pointers. I talk to most students once, but I focus more on Lue. He's an athlete. With more training, he could turn pro and become an MMA champion.

"Nong, over here please," Mr. Hodge yells.

I jog over to Mr. Hodge, who stands by his office. "When do you think you'll be ready to train again?" Mr. Matsuda stands next to him. Both of them have their arms crossed.

"The doctor said maybe in about six weeks it will be healed, but I can train now."

"Not with broken fingers you can't," Mr. Matsuda says.

"Well, this kind of training. Helping other students," I explain. When I help out with the students, I try to model May Li and how she tutored me. It was as much about building my confidence and fighting my fears as it was about understanding the material.

"True. But I guess what I want to know is, do you want to fight again?"

"Of course, as soon as you think I'm ready," I say.

"That's a good attitude," Mr. Hodge says. "But in the meantime, let's have you keep helping out."

"I've always had a good attitude," I say with a smile. Mr. Matsuda frowns.

"No, Nong, you've just had an attitude," Mr. Matsuda says. "But I think you're growing out of it. You always had the skills, but you were your own worst enemy."

I nod, although that's not quite the truth. My own worst enemy wasn't Nong Vang—it was the Ninja Warrior. He lost his first and only fight, and now he's retired to make room for Nong Vang to taste the sweet tea of victory.

CHAPTER 20

"Close the distance, Lue, close the distance!"

Lue bullies his way into a clinch. Lue threads his fingers in a perfect Muay Thai clinch and delivers hard knee shots that knock the wind out of his foe.

"Work, Lue, work!"

Lue continues to throw knees, then drops down, changes levels, and pulls his opponent to ground. Once on the ground, Lue fights for position.

"Get the mount!"

Lue fights through his foe's attempt to get guard and gets mount. From the mount, he uses elbows and punches, but with little effect.

"Look for it, look for it!"

Lue's foe is squirming on the ground, trying to get free, which allows Lue to pass guard. But rather than standing, Lue attacks his opponent with elbows while getting himself in position.

"Now!"

Lue spins his hips out so he's almost sitting next to his foe. One last elbow breaks down the defense, which allows Lue to encircle his foe's head in a head-lock position and then grab his wrist, bending the arm upwards. Lue quickly maneuvers his arm through the "hole" created by the bent wrist, then locks his own wrist. Squeezing hard, Lue instantly feels the tap on his leg.

After the match, the UFC announcer interviews Lue in the ring as his trainer straps the title belt around his waist. "Lue Vang, that was a great performance. Congratulations."

"Thanks Joe. Discipline in the dojo and aggression in the cage. That's the formula."

"That was quite a submission. You're becoming a complete fighter."

"I owe everything I am as a fighter to my trainer, my friend, my cuz, Nong Vang."

APPENDIX
MMA TERMS

Brazilian jiu-jitsu (BJJ): a martial art that focuses on grappling, in particular fighting on the ground; also called Gracie jiu-jitsu

choke: any hold used by a fighter around an opponent's throat with the goal of submission. A blood choke cuts off the supply of blood to the brain, while an air choke restricts oxygen. Types of choke holds include rear naked (applied from behind), guillotine (applied from in front), and triangle (applied from the ground).

dojo: a Japanese term meaning "place of the way," once used for temples but now more commonly used for gyms or schools where martial arts are taught

guard: a position on the mat where the fighter on his or her back uses his or her body to guard against an opponent's offensive moves by controlling the foe's body

jiu-jitsu: a Japanese-based martial art that uses no weapons and focuses less on strikes and more on grappling

Kimura: a judo submission hold. Its technical name is ude-garami, but it is usually referred to by the name of its inventor, Japanese judo master Masahiko Kimura.

mount: a dominant position where one fighter is on the ground and the other is on top

Muay Thai: a martial art from Thailand using striking and clinches. It is often referred to as the art of eight limbs for its use of right and left knees, fists, elbows, and feet.

savate: the French sport of kickboxing

shoot: in amateur wrestling, to attempt to take an opponent down

sprawl: a strategy to avoid takedowns by shooting the legs back or moving away from a foe

submission: any hold used to end a fight when one fighter surrenders (taps out) because the hold causes pain or risk of injury

takedown: an offensive move to take an opponent to the mat. Takedowns include single leg, double leg, and underhooks.

tap: the motion a fighter uses to show he or she is surrendering. A fighter can tap either the mat or his opponent with a hand.

TKO: technical knockout. A fighter who is not knocked out but can no longer defend himself or herself is "technically" knocked out, and the referee will stop the fight.

UFC: Ultimate Fighting Championship, the largest, most successful mixed martial arts promotion in the world since its beginning in 1993

MMA WEIGHT CLASSES

Flyweight	under 125.9 pounds
Bantamweight	126–134.9 pounds
Featherweight	135–144.9 pounds
Lightweight	145–154.9 pounds
Welterweight	155–169.9 pounds
Middleweight	170–184.9 pounds
Light Heavyweight	185–204.9 pounds
Heavyweight	205–264.9 pounds
Super Heavyweight	over 265 pounds

WELCOME TO the DOJO

BODY SHOT

PATRICK JONES

SIDE CONTROL

PATRICK JONES

LEARN TO FIGHT,
LEARN TO LIVE,
AND LEARN
TO FIGHT
FOR YOUR
LIFE.

HEAD KICK

PATRICK JONES

TRIANGLE CHOKE

PATRICK JONES

SOUTHSIDE HIGH

ARE YOU A SURVIVOR?

THE Alliance

Bad Deal

Beaten

Benito Runs

Dance Team

Deadly Drive

The Fight

Full Impact

Overexposed

Plan B

Recruited

Shattered Star

check out all the books in the

SURVIVING SOUTH SIDE

collection

ABOUT THE AUTHOR

Patrick Jones is the author of numerous novels for teens, including the Dojo series, as well as the nonfiction books *The Main Event: The Moves and Muscle of Pro Wrestling* and *Ultimate Fighting: The Brains and Brawn of Mixed Martial Arts* from Millbrook Press. A former librarian for teenagers, he received a lifetime achievement award from the American Library Association in 2006. He lives in Minneapolis but still considers Flint, Michigan, his hometown. He can be found on the web at www.connectingya.com and in front of his TV most weekends, watching UFC and WWE pay-per-views.